The Adventures of Sam Pig

Sam Pig and the Cuckoo Clock
Alison Uttley

Illustrated by Graham Percy

faber and faber

LONDON · BOSTON

First published in 1940
by Faber and Faber Limited
3 Queen Square London WC1N 3AU
This edition first published in 1989
Phototypeset by
Input Typesetting Ltd, London
Printed in Great Britain by
W. S. Cowell Ltd, Ipswich

A CIP record for this book is available
from the British Library.

ISBN 0–571–15468–9

Sam Pig and the Cuckoo Clock

On the mantelpiece in the house of the four pigs stood a clock, with a white face covered with a glass window, a brass pendulum and a hole for winding up the works. It was Badger's duty as head of the household to wind it, and nobody else ever dared to touch it. There it stood between Badger's herbbaccy box and the money-box with the slit for pence. Every night Badger lifted it down and opened the glass window. He took the key from its hook and then wound up the clock with a whirring clicking noise which always pleased little Sam Pig.

'Can I have a go, Brock? Can I wind up the clock? Can I look inside at the works?' he implored, but Brock shook his head.

'Nobody must wind it but me, for clocks are ticklish creatures, and they don't like clumsy paws meddling with their innards.'

The clock ticked with a cheerful sound, and the four pigs loved to listen to the familiar voice, saying 'Tick tock', night and day, and to watch the little brass pendulum which they could see through the glass window. It seemed to talk to them, to say, 'Now it's time to put the potatoes in the hot ashes to cook for dinner', or 'Now it's time to fill the kettle for tea'. They ran to obey.

When Badger went away for his winter's sleep the clock stopped, just as if it were lonely without him. The little pigs looked up at the white face, and listened for the tick, but the hands said 'A quarter to five', and they never moved day or night. Two friends were gone, Brock and the clock, and they missed them. When Badger returned, the first thing he did was to wind up the clock and start the little wagging pendulum. Then the clock called 'Here I am! Here I am!' and the four pigs rejoiced.

Of course there were plenty of ways of telling the

time besides the clock, but they were quiet ways. There was the sun moving majestically across the sky from East to West, sending shadows which got shorter and shorter till midday when they were the shortest. Then they began to lengthen till the sun went down. Badger put a stick in the garden and showed the family how to tell the time by it. He pointed to the stick's black shadow, which became only a very tiny fellow. 'The sun is the best clock of all,' said Brock. But sometimes the sun didn't shine and then there were no shadows.

Ann Pig said a good way to know the time was to pick a dandelion clock and blow the little white seedlings. 'One, two, three, four,' she puffed, and away flew the parasols to make new dandelions in the garden ready for salad.

Sam Pig liked a ticking clock, one that struck the hours and told everybody the time. He liked the brassy voice, and the loud call. So when the clock stopped and nobody was allowed to wind it up, Sam was very sad.

One day he climbed on a chair and reached for the clock. He fitted the key in the hole and turned it with a grinding noise. Clicketty Click went the clock, and Sam pressed it to his chest and dragged the key round and round with all his strength. He went on turning for a long time, and the clock didn't like the pain in its stomach. When Sam put the clock down there was a whirring buzz, and it began to strike. One, two, three, four, five, it went on striking all the hours and many more. It went into tomorrow and the next day. The hands whirled round and the clock ticked so madly that nobody knew what it said.

Ann was in a terrible fright when she heard it chattering like a cageful of magpies. Bill said the clock was saying, 'You shouldn't have done it. You shouldn't have done it. You shouldn't have done it.' Tom said that Badger would rage when he came home.

All the pigs ran about very fast, trying to go to bed, to get up, to eat and cook and do the work, but they couldn't keep up with the hastening clock. Ann was breathless, and Sam didn't know where he was. Tom burnt the dinner and let the kettle boil dry. The fire flared up in a fury, and the sticks crackled and spat. Everyone was in such a hurry and such a confusion that they fell on top of each other.

Only Bill sat in a corner watching the whirling fingers of the clock.

'It can't go on for ever like this,' he told them calmly, when Ann cried to him to hurry for it was tomorrow fortnight. 'It will be the end of the world soon, so we may as well take it easy while we can.'

'The end of the world?' Ann burst into tears. 'I won't have my end of the world without Brock,' she sobbed.

Then Sam went into the garden, scampering out and scampering in at double speed.

'The shadow-stick is moving quite slowly,' said he. 'The sun isn't running across the sky. It's the same as usual. It's only today. I think something's going to happen to this clock.'

Sure enough the clock struck one thousand, one hundred and one. It whirred and buzzed and chuffed. Then it was silent. Never was there such a silence. The four pigs stood staring, motionless. The birds in the garden stopped singing, and even the wind was quiet as if it couldn't understand what had happened in the house of the four pigs.

Then everyone began to talk. The birds sang, the wind whistled and all the pigs shouted, 'It's broken. Time has stopped.' They asked each other what Badger would say! They were very much upset! They looked inside the clock and touched its snapped springs, and its toothed wheels and its slim fingers.

'We had best get another clock before Brock comes home,' said Bill.

'But where shall we find one?' asked Tom.

'We are the only family that has a clock,' said Ann.

'And there may not be another in all the world,' said Bill.

'Oh, yes! I've seen clocks on church towers,' interrupted Sam eagerly.

'All right, Sam. You'd best get a clock from a church tower,' said Tom, coldly. 'You broke our clock, and you seem to know all about them. You go and get one.'

Sam's face fell. 'I can't climb a church tower,' he explained. 'It's miles and miles high, and when you get to the top the church clock is as big as a house. We could all live inside a clock like that, we should be deafened by the striking.'

'That's your affair,' said Bill crossly. 'You broke the clock and you must get another from somewhere.'

'Yes. That's fair enough,' said Tom. Only Ann was sorry for the little pig who stood looking so disconsolate.

'Never mind, Sam,' she whispered. 'I'll say a word to Brock and he will forgive you.'

'Forgiving won't give us back our clock,' said Bill, who overheard. 'Now, Ann, leave him alone. He must go off and find a clock.'

'And he mustn't come back with a dandelion clock either,' added Tom, sternly.

So Sam packed his pyjamas in his knapsack, and

a piece of soap and a toothbrush with them. Ann gave him a rock bun and a clean handkerchief, and away he went clock-hunting.

But clocks don't grow on oak trees, and although Sam searched high and low in the woods he couldn't find anything like a clock. The Jay watched him and hopped from bough to bough of the trees to try to find what Sam Pig was looking for. The wood pigeons called, 'Tak two coos, Sam. Tak two coos,' but that didn't help. The cuckoo called, 'Cuckoo. Cuckoo,' and flew over Sam's head.

'Has anybody seen a clock?' called Sam Pig, but the birds only whistled and sang with joy because Spring had come with the cuckoo.

So Sam Pig sat down and ate his cake and thought it over. He couldn't go back without a clock, so he decided to go to an old friend for advice. He decided to visit the old witch, who wasn't a witch at all, but an old woman who lived alone in the wood.

That was a good plan, he was sure, and he sprang to his feet and started off through the long deep woods towards the little cottage. It was late at night when he arrived, but the old woman had a candle burning in her window and a bright fire blazing on her hearth. The light of it flickered down the wood among the trees, and Sam hastened to the garden and up to the door. He tapped and waited.

'Come in. Come in, whoever you may be,' said the witch.

'Why, it's my little Pigwiggin come to see me again,' she cried when Sam pushed open the door and stepped into the room, blinking at the light.

She threw her arms around Sam Pig and kissed him on the nose.

'How are you, little Pigwiggin?' she cried.

Sam said he was very well, only tired and hungry. So she gave him supper and aired his pyjamas, and all the time she talked to him about her Owlet and her cat. The Owlet was now full grown, she told Sam, and he no longer rode on her shoulder, he was too heavy. He sat on a chair and stared with round eyes at Sam Pig. As for the cat she turned her back and took no notice whatever.

'And what brings you here?' asked the old woman at last when Sam had said nothing. 'I hope you haven't run away from home.'

'No, although I sometimes want to when Bill and Tom are angry with me,' said Sam fiercely. 'No. They turned me out.'

'What? Packed you off into the wide world?'

'Yes. They sent me away,' said Sam.

'But why? What have you done?' asked the witch, sorrowfully.

'I broke our clock,' said Sam, 'and they sent me out to find another.'

Then he told her how he had wound up Badger's clock, which went buzzing along till it broke.

'Do you know where I can find a clock?' asked Sam. 'I came to ask you, because you are the wisest person I know, except Brock.'

He looked anxiously at the witch over the edge of his bowl of milk. There was a comforting ticking sound in the room, and he knew the witch had a clock for he had seen it on his first visit.

'You've come to the right place, Pigwiggin,' said the witch. 'I've got a clock I never use, for it makes such a to-do, such a chatter, I get weary of it. I want to be quiet in my old age. You shall have it with pleasure, for there is the old grandfather clock in the corner, and he keeps me company. I don't want my little noisy clock.'

Sam thanked her over and over again, but she stopped him.

'That's enough, Sam. You've said "Thank you" as often as a striking clock. Say no more but go off to sleep. Tomorrow I will get the clock down from the attic. It's a queer one but it keeps good time, and you can wind it yourself.'

So she made up the bed on the hearthrug, and Sam lay down in his warm pyjamas. Just before he fell asleep he heard the old woman call 'Tirra-lirra', and a mouse ran out of a hole to be fed. Sam smiled sleepily at the Owl and nodded at the sulky cat. Then he shut his eyes and knew no more till morning.

The next day they all had breakfast together of porridge and cream. The porridge had curls of treacle on the top.

'What's this?' asked Sam. 'What is this sweetness that isn't honey?' He had never seen treacle before of course, for it comes from the sugar-cane, and not from the honeycomb.

'It's treacle, my Pigwiggin,' said the old woman. 'Have you never tasted it before? You shall have a tin to take home with you.'

'It's delicious,' said Sam. 'Even the bees would desert their honey-tree for this tin, I think, and the Fox would run a mile for a taste.'

The old woman nodded and smiled and gave him more till his buttons were nearly bursting off. Then she took him into the garden to see her daffodils and pinks. It was such a warm sunny corner of the forest that the flowers all bloomed at once and they kept in blossom till the snows came.

Overhead flew the Jay. 'Witch! Witch!' he shrieked, and he swooped down to snatch a crust from the bird-table which the old woman had set for him and his friends.

'Pretty Jay,' she said. 'He comes here every day to see me, and he always speaks so kindly to me.'

Sam Pig frowned at the Jay, and the Jay mocked and jeered at Sam Pig.

But the old woman went back to the house and brought out the clock. It was a most beautiful clock in the shape of a little house, with a window just under the thatched roof, and the clock face over the front door. Two fir cones dangled from beneath it and the old woman showed Sam how to wind it up. She pulled down one fir cone, and the other moved into the house. It was quite easy, and the clock at once began to tick in a loud and cheerful manner.

'Put it under your arm,' said the witch. 'Don't jerk it, but carry it carefully, and when you get home ask your brother to hang it on the wall. It is going now and will tell you the time all the way home.'

Sam thanked her again and away he went, with the clock under one arm and the tin of treacle under the other.

The old woman stood at her gate waving to him till he got out of sight.

'The good little Pigwiggin,' said she to herself.

Sam trotted along towards home, and he hummed a song of happiness because he was carrying a clock for Brock the Badger. The clock ticked loudly against his heart, and the treacle tin sent out a good sweet smell.

'It's a very pretty clock,' said Sam, taking a peep at it. 'They will be surprised when they see it. A house with two fir cones!'

There was a sudden whir and the little window flew open. Out flew a tiny cuckoo and shouted, 'Cuckoo. Cuckoo. Cuckoo,' nine times. Then back it flew and the window shut and the clock went on ticking as if nothing had happened.

'Goodness me!' cried Sam, holding the clock at arm's length. 'There's a cuckoo inside it! And it knows the time, for it *is* nine o'clock!'

He hurried along the woods, but every hour the cuckoo came out and sang its merry song and fluttered its little feathers. Sam tried to catch it, to make it speak of other things, but the cuckoo flew back to the dark interior of the clock and shut the window fast.

'Ho, cuckoo! Stop a minute!' called Sam. 'Let me in! Open your window! I want to look inside your house.' He rapped at the door and tapped at the window, and peered down the chimney, but he could see nothing.

'Tick tock! Tick tock!' went the clock, and the house door remained firmly closed.

'Why are you hurrying so fast, Sam Pig?' asked the Fox, stepping out of the bushes. 'What have you got there?'

'Nothing for you,' said Sam quickly, and he tried to push past, but the Fox snatched the clock from him.

'A house,' said the Fox. 'And who lives in it, Sam? Some honey-bees perhaps. There is a sweet smell about you, Sam Pig.' Sam Pig had pushed the tin of treacle in his pocket, and now he stood waiting.

'Tick tock!' went the clock, very loudly, and then

it made a little buzzing noise.

'I think it is going to explode,' said the Fox, holding it at arm's length. 'I think this house is a queer one.'

Out flew the cuckoo, and shouted, 'Cuckoo. Cuckoo,' in the Fox's face, and flapped its little wings against his nose.

'The bold bird! Take it back! I don't want such a magical thing. It's a trap or something. You take care, Sam Pig, or that bird will peck your eyes out. It nearly got mine.'

So Sam Pig went home with the cuckoo clock safe and sound, and the Fox ran through the woods to tell his family that Sam Pig had a magical bird in a little magical house, and it would peck your eyes out as soon as winking.

The pigs were delighted when Sam showed them the new clock, and they hung it up on a nail in the kitchen. They all stood listening to the noisy tick tock, and gazing at the little house. The roof was thatched with green reeds, and the little door had a brass knocker. Sam explained that he had knocked and banged at the door and tapped on the window but nobody came out till it was the hour for striking.

'It's four o'clock,' said he. 'Now you shall see for yourselves.'

The window sprang open and out flew the little cuckoo, and called the hour.

It flew round the room, calling, 'Cuckoo.Cuckoo!' It blinked its eyes and shook its feathers and tossed its head, and then it returned to the little house.

The pigs could talk of nothing else all evening, and as each hour approached they waited for the bird to come out and sing to them. It was striking eight when Badger entered the room.

'Hallo,' he cried. 'What's this? A little cuckoo

flying round? Where has it come from? It's the smallest bird I ever saw in all my life.'

But the bird flicked its tail, called eight times and flew back through its window.

'It's a clock,' said Sam. 'I broke your clock, Brock. This is a new one, from the witch's house. It's a cuckoo clock.'

Brock stood looking at the little house, admiring the neat thatching of the roof, and the overlapping wooden shingles, and the sweet-scented fir cones

which hung from their chains. Then he lifted the brass knocker and tapped at the tiny door.

'It's no good knocking there,' said Sam. 'It's not a real door. Nothing happens.'

But even as he spoke the door swung slowly open and they could see inside the little house. There was the cuckoo, sitting in a bare little room, with its feathers drooping and its shoulders hunched. It glanced at them, and then turned its head away.

'Hush,' said Sam Pig. 'It's going to sleep,' and they closed the door.

But early the next morning Sam Pig slipped down to the kitchen, and waited to see the cuckoo come out. It darted from its window and flew cuckooing out of the door, and into the woods. Away it flew, and it didn't come back for an hour. With it came another cuckoo, small and stiff like itself, with quick bright eyes and grey-barred breast. They both flew in at the little window of the cuckoo clock, and the shutter closed after them.

'There's another cuckoo come to the clock,' said Sam, when Brock came down to breakfast. 'I expect our cuckoo was lonely.'

Brock tapped at the door and pushed it open a crack. There were primroses on the table, and on the hearth a little fire gleamed. Two cuckoos sat talking by the fireside, speaking in low whispering voices.

Brock closed the door silently and nodded to Sam.

'Did you see the little fire burning and the candle-stick on the mantelpiece and the primroses?' asked Sam.

'Yes. Look at the smoke coming out of the chimney. The cuckoo is making himself at home.'

Indeed it was so, for a tiny column of blue smoke came curling from the chimney of the wooden house. Every hour the cuckoo came out to call the time, and with him came his wife, two birds which flew round the room and then disappeared into their own little dwelling.